BUGS BUNNY™
in
Escape From Noddington Castle

By Kennon Graham

Illustrated by Darrell Baker

GOLDEN PRESS

Western Publishing Company, Inc.
Racine, Wisconsin

Copyright © 1980 by Warner Bros. Inc. All rights reserved.
No part of this book may be reproduced or copied in any form without written permission from the publisher.
Printed in the U.S.A. by Western Publishing Company, Inc.
Golden®, A Golden Book® and Golden Press® are trademarks of Western Publishing Company, Inc.
BUGS BUNNY is the Trademark of Warner Bros. Inc. used under License.
Library of Congress Cataloging in Publication Data
Harrison, David Lee, 1937—
Bugs Bunny in Escape from Noddington Castle. [1. Adventure stories. 2. Animals—Fiction] I. Baker, Darrell. II. Title.
PZ7.H2474Bu   [E]   80-13646
Library of Congress Catalog Number: 80-51547   ISBN 0-307-10827-9
CDEFGHIJ

"Hurry up, Bugs," said Porky Pig. "The museum guide's getting to the best part of the tour."

Bugs Bunny yawned. "Can't hurry. After that Deluxe Double Carrot-Burger lunch, I need a nap."

"But, Bugs," Porky said, "the guide's talking about kings and queens and knights and castles!"

"Tell me about it later, pal," said Bugs. "Right now I'm cruisin' for some snoozin'."

Bugs found a cushion in a quiet corner. He snuggled up and soon was sleeping. But suddenly...

"Help!" yelled Porky.

Bugs sat up with a jolt. He was surprised to see a knight in armor pointing a sword at him.

"Follow me," ordered the knight. "I arrest you in the name of the king of Noddington Castle."

The knight led them through the dark and musty
corridors of the castle to the Throne Room.

"Enter and bow before King Robert and Queen Anne,"
said the knight.

Porky bowed elegantly. He had never met a real
king and queen before, and he was very impressed.
But Bugs had a different approach.

"Hiya, pal," Bugs said to the king. "What's up, doc?"

"Why've we been arrested?" asked Porky.

"You have been arrested for trespassing," the king said sternly. "To the dungeon with you both!"

"Now hold on here, Kingsy," said Bugs. "Couldn't we make a deal? What if we work to earn our freedom? There must be something we could do."

"Can you cook?" asked the queen.

"Can we cook?" cried Bugs. "Why, my dee-licious Creamy Carrot Soup is world famous!"

"Good," said the queen. "We'll try it tonight."

Bugs and Porky cooked all afternoon. First they filled a pot with carrots and water. Then Bugs threw in salt, molasses, hot peppers, and beets.

"Are you sure you know what you're doing?" asked Porky as he watched Bugs pour a whole jar of vinegar into the pot.

"Of course I'm sure," Bugs said. "The royal couple will be begging for my recipe."

That evening, Bugs and Porky proudly carried
the Creamy Carrot Soup to the royal dining table.

"It has an interesting aroma," said the queen.

"It has an interesting color," said the king.

They raised their spoons. They sipped their
soup. They dropped their spoons.

"We've been poisoned!" cried the king. "Guard!
Guard! Away with these scoundrels!"

The knight marched the prisoners to the stable.
"Clean out all the stalls," he commanded.
"Feed the horses and take special care with the
king's favorite steed, Thunderbolt. And have all
the horses saddled first thing tomorrow morning,
for the fox hunt." Then he turned and left.

Porky started sweeping and Bugs fed Thunderbolt.
Then Bugs climbed into the hayloft and flopped down.

"No resting, Bugs," said Porky. "Are you trying
to get us thrown into the dungeon?"

"Relax, partner," answered Bugs. "There'll be
plenty of time to finish this job tomorrow. We'll
get an early start and do it before the king and
queen get here. Right now I'm hitting the hay."

But the next morning Bugs and Porky were still
snoring when the royal hunting party arrived. The
stable was a mess and the horses weren't saddled.

The king was furious. He shook his fist. "Where
are those good-for-nothing prisoners?" he roared.

The king's bellowing woke Bugs and Porky.

"We'd better hide here until the king simmers down," Bugs whispered.

But just then Porky's nose began to twitch. "Bugs," he said desperately, "I'm...I'm going to sneeze. Ah-Ah-CHOO!"

Porky's sneeze blasted Bugs out of the hayloft.

Bugs landed on King Robert's head. King Robert staggered backwards and grabbed Thunderbolt's tail to steady himself. Startled, Thunderbolt charged out of the stable—with King Robert holding on for dear life.

"Take these troublemakers to the dungeon!" yelled the queen.

"Uh-oh. We're in for it now," groaned Porky.

"Stop worrying," said Bugs. "I'll save us."

He turned to the king and queen. "Your Royal Majesties, I'm surprised at you. Haven't you recognized me yet? I'm the famous Bugs Le Bunnee, Magician Extraordinaire."

The king looked suspicious. He sent for his court magician, Gargoyle the Great.

"Investigate this Bugs Le Bunnee character," the king said. "Find out if he really is a magician."

So Gargoyle asked to see Bugs' tricks.

Bugs held up a coin in his right hand. "Hocus pocus, carrot tocus," he chanted. He clapped and—zip!—suddenly the coin was in his other hand.

"Wow," said Porky, but Gargoyle was not impressed. He held up a coin, too. Then he wiggled his beard.

Instantly the coin became a rooster...

then a frog...

then a block of ice.

Finally it vanished in a puff of smoke!

"That's nothing," sniffed Bugs. "Watch this."

He was sure no one in Noddington had ever seen
matches. He held one up. "Here is a perfectly ordinary
twig," he declared. "Now observe." He struck the match
against a rock. The match burst into flame.

Gargoyle smiled. He blew on his cane. Huge purple
flames shot into the air.

Then Gargoyle snapped his fingers. A tiny
purring kitten changed into a giant snarling tiger.

"Beginner's luck," said Bugs. "Kid stuff. But
no one has ever done what I'm about to do."

The king and queen looked interested.

"I can turn a broken-down old nag into the
fastest steed in all the kingdom! Assistant," he said
to Porky, "bring me a horse."

Bugs whispered instructions in Porky's ear.
Porky hurried to the stable. He soon returned
riding a beautiful, sleek horse.

"Why, that's my Thunderbolt!" cried the king.
"He already *is* the fastest horse in the kingdom!"

"I was hoping you'd say that, Kingsy," Bugs
chuckled as he hopped up behind Porky. "For my
last trick, I'm going to make us disappear!"

And he and Porky galloped away.

An army of knights chased after them. But
Thunderbolt really was the fastest horse of all.
In no time, he had carried Bugs and Porky to the
far edge of Noddington Kingdom.

"Thanks for the lift, old chum," Bugs said to
Thunderbolt. "You head back now. We'll find our
way home from here."

KINGDOM
LIMITS

Bugs was just wondering if he'd ever see
Thunderbolt again when...

"Wake up, Bugs!" Porky called.

"Huh?" said Bugs sleepily. He opened his eyes.
He wasn't in Noddington Kingdom. He was still in
the museum. He had fallen asleep!

Bugs and Porky rejoined the tour. The guide was
pointing to a painting. "This is King Robert of
Noddington, seen here atop his favorite horse."

KING ROBERT

"Thunderbolt!" Bugs cried.

The guide's mouth fell open. "How did you know
the horse's name?" he asked.

"That's a long story, doc," Bugs said, "and you
probably wouldn't believe it if I told you."

Bugs Bunny winked at the painting of Thunderbolt.
And although he couldn't be certain, he thought he
saw Thunderbolt wink back.